Locked in the Library!

A Marc Brown ARTHUR Chapter Book

Locked in the Library!

Little, Brown and Company

Boston   New York   London

First Edition

The characters and events portrayed in this book are fictitious. Any
similarity to real persons, living or dead, is coincidental and not
intended by the author.

Arthur® is a registered trademark of Marc Brown.

Text by Stephen Krensky, based on the teleplay by Kathy Waugh

Text has been reviewed and assigned a reading level by
Laurel S. Ernst, M.A., Teachers College, Columbia University,
New York, New York; reading specialist, Chappaqua, New York

ISBN 0-316-11557-6 (hc)
ISBN 0-316-12190-8 (pb)

Library of Congress Catalog Card Number 97-75973

10 9 8 7 6 5 4 3

WOR (hc)
COM-MO (pb)

Printed in the United States of America

For the Quadri crew:
Colleen, Hayley, and Shea

Chapter 1

· · · · · · · · · · ·

Arthur and Buster were walking up the
school steps one morning when an angry
voice shouted behind them, "ARTHUR!
ARTHUR READ!"

Arthur turned.

Buster turned, too.

The voice belonged to Francine. She was
charging toward them. Muffy and Sue
Ellen were with her.

"What's up?" asked Arthur.

Francine folded her arms. "I'll tell you
what's up. You told everyone I looked like
a marshmallow."

"I did?"

Buster nodded. "Don't you remember, Arthur? She was wearing that goofy sweater, the one that puffs up everywhere."

"Oh, *that* sweater." Arthur remembered it now. It had padded shoulders and wool that fluffed out like frosting.

"You'd better say you're sorry," said Francine.

"Or what?" said Buster.

Francine ignored Buster and stared Arthur in the eye.

"Or else you're going to get it."

"Oh, yeah?" said Buster. "You can't talk to Arthur that way."

Francine tossed her head and continued up the steps.

Muffy and Sue Ellen did the same.

"I guess we told *them*," said Buster.

" 'We'?" said Arthur.

"You don't have to thank me," said

Buster, putting his arm around Arthur's shoulders. "That's what friends are for."

Arthur just sighed.

A little while later, when he went into class, he could feel himself being glared at.

"This is all your fault," he said to Buster.

Buster wedged himself into Arthur's seat. "*My* fault?" he said. "You're the one who called Francine a marshmallow."

"And you're the one who talked so tough."

"I was just standing up for you."

"I think it might be better if I stood up for myself."

A folded note flew through the air and landed on Arthur's desk. He unfolded it and read it aloud quietly.

"*This is your final warning. You are —*"

Buster grabbed the note out of Arthur's hand.

"*. . . in big trouble,*" he continued. "*And I*

mean BIG." He paused. "I think that's a skull and crossbones." He stopped to think. "That's not a good sign."

Arthur turned around and looked at Francine. She was still glaring at him. Muffy and Sue Ellen were glaring at him, too.

"Attention, please!" said the teacher, Mr. Ratburn, from the front of the room. "Buster, perhaps you would consider taking your own seat."

Buster pulled himself out of Arthur's chair and zipped back to his own.

"Now," Mr. Ratburn continued, standing at the blackboard, "let's get started. Have you ever wondered what makes a hero or heroine? Are people born brave and generous, or do they become this way later on?"

The kids all looked at one another. They were puzzled. Were they supposed to answer the question, or was Mr. Ratburn just talking to himself? He did that sometimes.

"Anyway," Mr. Ratburn went on, "that's what I want you to think about this weekend."

Everyone groaned.

"Please prepare an oral report on the hero or heroine of your choice. You'll be working in pairs." Mr. Ratburn consulted his notes. "Binky, you're with Sue Ellen. Muffy, you'll be working with Buster." He named some other pairs. "And Arthur, you're teamed with Francine."

Arthur glanced at Francine. She looked like she was going to die.

He sighed. It was going to be a very long weekend.

Chapter 2

• • • • • • • • • • •

Heroes and heroines. That's what Arthur and Buster talked about on their way home from school.

"Who's your favorite?" Buster asked. "I mean, there are a lot of heroes to choose from. I know we're studying the ones from real life. But what about Robin Hood or Hercules?"

"Or the Bionic Bunny," said Arthur.

Buster nodded. "Exactly," he said.

Arthur wasn't sure he had a favorite. He had always liked reading stories about heroes, but he had never thought much about what made them the way they were or which ones he liked best.

"You know what I really like about heroes?" said Buster.

"What?"

"Well, that they're so heroic, so brave. I wish I could do half the things they do."

"Me, too," said Arthur. He paused. "Do you think heroes ever call their friends marshmallows?"

Buster wasn't sure. "I know one thing. If they do, they don't worry about it later."

Arthur nodded. It would certainly help things if he could be a little more heroic himself.

When Arthur got home, he found D.W. talking on the kitchen phone.

"He said *what?*" D.W. gasped.

She listened for a moment.

"I can't believe it," she went on. "Well, I

suppose I can. Nothing Arthur does really surprises me."

She glared at her brother.

Arthur shook his head. He was being glared at a lot lately.

"Who are you talking to?" he asked.

D.W. ignored him. "Uh-huh . . . Well, he should talk. Guess what he looks like in his pajamas? . . . No . . . No, but I like that one. Give up?"

"D.W.!" Arthur shouted.

"A dumpling. He looks like a soggy dumpling."

Arthur reached for the phone.

D.W. held up her hand to stop him. "Okay," she said. "I'll tell him. Bye."

She hung up the phone.

"Wasn't that for me?" said Arthur.

"Yes and no." D.W. smiled. "I have to give you the message because Francine isn't talking to you."

"She's not?"

D.W. laughed. "You can't go around calling someone a marshmallow and expect her not to care."

"I didn't know it was such a big deal," said Arthur. "I mean, I like marshmallows."

D.W. was not impressed. "To eat, maybe, but not to look like."

Arthur rolled his eyes. "So what was the message?" he asked.

"Francine says to meet her at the library tomorrow at three. But you can't speak to her because she's not speaking to you."

Arthur sighed.

D.W. stuck her nose in the air. "And I don't blame her."

"But how are we supposed to get any work done if we're not speaking?"

D.W. wagged her finger at him. "You should have thought of that before you started calling people names."

And with that, D.W. went upstairs, leaving Arthur thinking that if he were a hero, he wouldn't be in this mess.

Chapter 3

● ● ● ● ● ● ● ● ● ● ●

The next afternoon, Arthur ran up the steps of the Elwood City library just as the clock struck three.

Phew, he thought.

He had been playing in the backyard with Pal and had lost track of the time. So he had needed to hurry. If Francine had to wait for him, that would just give her something else to complain about.

Inside the library, Arthur saw the librarian, Ms. Turner, standing by the reference desk. Francine was with her.

"Hello, Ms. Turner," he said.

The librarian looked up from the book she was consulting. She smiled.

"Good afternoon, Arthur. Francine was just telling me about your report."

Arthur had hoped that Francine might have used up her glare by now. But as she turned toward him, he could see that it was still going strong.

"As I was saying," said Francine, "even though we're working on this report together, I'm in charge."

"Oh, really?" said Arthur. "I don't remember Mr. Ratburn saying anything about that."

Francine folded her arms. "Well, you just weren't listening closely enough. Probably too busy thinking up new insults."

"I was not!"

Francine turned away. "Of course, we're not going to discuss it further, because we're not speaking to each other."

"Francine, that's the most—"

"Heroes can be so inspirational," Ms. Turner put in. "Don't you agree, Arthur? Francine was just telling me some of her ideas. What sort of hero are you looking for?"

"Well," said Arthur, trying to get himself under control. "Let's see. Someone heroic, of course."

"Ooooh!" said Francine. "Good thought, Arthur."

Arthur turned a little red. "I'm just thinking out loud. He might be—"

"What about a *she?*" said Francine.

"Okay," said Arthur. "A woman is fine as long as she did something famous."

Ms. Turner tapped her pencil on the counter. "How about Joan of Arc?" she said. "She was certainly famous, and one of the youngest leaders in history. She was an inspiration, leading the French army in battle against the English invaders. Her story has battles, horses—exciting stuff. I believe we have books about her in the European History section as well as in the biographies."

"I'll take biographies," Arthur and Francine said together.

They stared at each other.

"I called it first!" said Francine.

"You did not!'

"Did, too!"

"Goodness, children," said Ms. Turner. "It's nice to see such enthusiasm." She looked at their frowning faces. "But maybe I should decide. Francine, you were here first, so why don't you look in the biographies."

"Yes!" said Francine. She stuck out her tongue at Arthur.

"As for you, Arthur, you could try the stacks. Medieval French history is in the 940s. That's down the stairs and around the corner."

Arthur nodded.

Francine headed down the aisle.

"But don't forget," Ms. Turner called after them, "the library will close promptly at—"

"We know," said Francine. "Five o'clock."

Chapter 4

• • • • • • • • • • •

Arthur found a big book on French history at 940.21. He was impressed that Ms. Turner knew just where to send him without looking anything up. The library number system was confusing to him.

The book had a tapestry on the front, decorated with unicorns and women in long dresses. Inside, Arthur found a lot of information. Some of the French had conquered England in 1066, but by the early 1400s, much of France was under English control.

And the French didn't like that.

Holding the book in both hands, Arthur

settled onto a big, comfortable couch next to a grandfather clock. Then he started to read. There were tons of facts to get through. Before long, his eyelids grew heavy, and he slumped down against the cushion.

"Look out, Sir Arthur!" cried a voice from the battlement.

Arthur ducked as an arrow whizzed harmlessly over his head.

"Thank you, Lord Buster!" he called out.

"We are lucky the French have such poor aim," said Lord Buster.

"True," said Sir Arthur. "But I fear they plan to do a lot of practicing."

From his perch, Arthur looked out over the field of battle. The French army had gathered in great force outside the moat.

Sir Arthur shook his head. All this had happened just because he had called the French *general a marshmallow. She had taken great offense at that.*

He regretted the comment now, but he was too proud to admit it. Besides, the French general didn't seem in the mood for apologies.

She was riding her horse back and forth in front of her troops.

"We will take the castle!" she was saying in French — although Arthur could somehow understand her.

Her army cheered.

"Then we will see who is the marshmallow around here."

Arthur heard the clock in the tower ringing out the hour. Bong, bong, bong, bong, bong. The day was growing late. Did the French still plan to attack — or would they wait until morning?

Up the stairs and around the corner, Francine had opened a chapter book about

Joan of Arc. It was nice and private here. As long as she stayed put, she wouldn't have to risk running into Arthur.

Francine sat down cross-legged and put on her Walkman. She had brought a tape to play while she read. That way, even if Arthur found her, she could easily ignore him.

The book itself was pretty interesting. It told of how Joan of Arc led the French army and defeated the English at Orléans. The Maid of Orléans, she was called. She was only about seventeen when she started fighting, but she got to wear armor and carry a sword.

Francine wondered about the armor. It must have been heavy. If Joan ever fell down, did she need help getting up?

Humming to the music, she kept reading as the light faded in the windows at the end of the aisle.

Chapter 5

Arthur yawned. He hadn't meant to fall asleep. The nap had just sneaked up on him. He stretched lazily. He had never thought of the library as a good place to sleep, but it certainly was quiet.

He stood up and walked back toward the main desk. The only sound he heard was his own footsteps. That seemed odd. The library was supposed to be quiet, of course, but this seemed *too quiet*.

"Ms. Turner?" Arthur called out.

Nobody answered.

Arthur looked around. A lot of the lights

were off. That was odd, too. He ran to the front door and pulled the handle.

The door was locked! Arthur shook it as hard as he could.

The door stayed locked.

Suddenly the grandfather clock began to chime.

Bong, bong, bong, bong, bong, bong!

Arthur was counting. Six bongs! That meant six o'clock. But the library closed at five. He distinctly remembered Ms. Turner mentioning that fact. That meant the library was . . . closed!

Arthur was scared. How could the library be closed? He was still inside it. Libraries weren't supposed to close with people inside them.

Arthur gulped. If he was inside by himself, that meant he was alone. Very alone.

Suddenly the library's familiar nooks

and crannies didn't look so friendly. Were those shadows moving across the floor to grab him? No, no, they were just the shadows of branches blown by the wind. What about the books, though? If he turned his back on them, would they fly off the shelves and hit him in the back?

Arthur squeezed his eyes shut. Stay calm, he told himself. It's only a library.

He opened one eye to take another look. Everything seemed normal. He opened the other. The shadows were minding their own business. The books hadn't moved from the stacks.

Crassshhh!

Arthur jumped. That sound was not his imagination. His imagination couldn't make up a noise like that.

Arthur bit his lip. Maybe he wasn't alone in the library. The thought should have made him feel better—but it didn't.

"Hello? Is anyone there?"

No one answered. Arthur walked along, looking around. Someone or something had made that crash. He had to find out more.

With his heart pounding in his chest, he took a few steps forward. He tried to walk silently, but the floor creaked under his sneakers.

When he reached the stairs, Arthur looked up and down the stairwell. Both directions looked dark and scary.

What would Joan of Arc have done in this situation? Arthur wondered. She at least would have been armed for battle. The only thing Arthur had to protect himself with was a pencil — and even that needed sharpening.

Arthur listened carefully. There had been no further crashes. Maybe the first one was a fluke, a pile of books that had

fallen over. Maybe he could relax a little —
and concentrate on getting out of the
library.

And then a hand grabbed his shoulder
from behind.

Chapter 6

• • • • • • • • • • • •

"Aagghh!" Arthur screamed. He whirled around.

"Aagghh!" Francine screamed back. She was standing right behind him.

The two of them just stood there, shaking for a moment.

"Why did you scream?" she cried.

"You screamed, too," said Arthur.

"Only because you screamed first."

Arthur took a deep breath. "Well, why shouldn't I scream? I'm alone in a dark library. I hear a crash—"

"That wasn't a crash," said Francine. "I

accidentally knocked some books off a desk. It barely made any noise at all."

"It sounded like a crash to me," Arthur insisted. "And then I go to investigate, and this creepy hand grabs me on the shoulder—"

"My hand isn't creepy," said Francine. "It's a very nice hand." She looked at it and smiled. Then her smile turned to a frown. "Anyway, what are you doing here?"

Arthur put his hands on his hips. "I could ask you the same question," he said.

Francine sighed. "I was looking for Ms. Turner. Then I heard the clock chiming. It's after six, you know."

"I can count, Francine."

She was not impressed. "So you say. But where were you an hour ago?"

"Looking through some books."

"Well, why didn't you come find me?

The library was closing. Five o'clock, remember? You got us locked in."

Arthur blushed. "I did not!"

"So then what happened?"

Arthur hesitated. "Well, actually, I fell asleep."

"Asleep!" Francine laughed. "You must feel pretty silly."

Arthur made a face. "Maybe I do, and maybe I don't. But at least I have an excuse. What about you? Since you remember the time so well, why didn't you come find *me*?"

Now it was Francine's turn to blush. "Okay, okay, I was listening to music while I looked through the books. I guess I didn't hear the clock, either."

"Ha! So you weren't paying any more attention than I was."

"Never mind that," said Francine. "I don't have time to argue with you. I have to get out of here."

"Fine," said Arthur. "Do you have a plan?"

"A plan?"

"A way to get out." Arthur frowned. "As you said, we're locked in."

"I'm working on one," she sniffed. "And when it's ready, I'll put it into operation. But I'm not going to share my ideas with you. Do you know why? Because I'm still not talking to you. And I'm not listening, either."

To make the point perfectly clear, Francine stuck her fingers in her ears and walked away.

Chapter 7

• • • • • • • • • • •

Even though Arthur and Francine were not working together, they both had the same idea about what to do next.

Maybe I can climb out a window, thought Arthur.

I think I'll try the window, thought Francine.

Arthur began piling up a rickety pile of books. When he was done, he began climbing up.

The pile swayed back and forth.

Arthur was about to grab the window handle when Francine came by. One of the books in Arthur's pile was exactly the size she needed to complete a nice, neat pile of her own.

She yanked out the book.

Arthur's pile fell down. Arthur hit the floor with a loud thud.

"You should build things more carefully," said Francine.

With the last book in place, Francine's pile was perfectly steady. She climbed up to the window and gave the latch a pull.

It was stuck.

She gave it a few tugs, but the latch didn't move.

A fly buzzed in front of her face.

"Go away!" said Francine. "Find your own way out."

She waved her hand wildly at the fly.

"Whoaaaa!" Francine landed with a crash.

Arthur came running around the corner and almost tripped over Francine, who was lying on the floor.

"What happened?" he asked.

Francine picked herself up. "I lost my balance," she said, forgetting that she wasn't talking to him.

"What about the window?"

Francine shook her head. "Forget it," she said. "I don't think these windows have been opened in a long time."

"Uh-oh!"

"What?" Francine snapped.

"I just remembered something," said Arthur. "Today is Saturday. That means the library is closed until—"

"Monday!" Francine finished for him. She gulped. "What's that noise?"

"What noise?"

"I hear growling."

Arthur looked down. "That's my stomach. It's thinking about getting no food for the entire weekend."

"We have more than your stomach to

worry about," said Francine. "Our families will be worried sick."

Arthur thought about how D.W. would take the news. He could picture her pulling down his posters, throwing out his toys, and painting the walls pink.

"Not everyone," he said.

"Wait a minute!" said Francine. "I've got it."

She ran to the card catalog and began flipping through the listings.

"Are you crazy?" said Arthur. "How is a *book* going to help us?"

Francine ignored him. "Let's see," she said. *"How to Escape from Prison, How to Escape from a Desert Island . . .* Aha!"

"Aha, what?" said Arthur.

"How to Escape from a Library, of course."

Arthur was impressed. He hadn't realized that this sort of thing happened so often.

"Hey! Wait for me!" he said, following Francine into the stacks.

She found the place for the book. It made a hole like the gap in a smile after a tooth has fallen out.

"I don't believe it! Who would need a book on escaping from a library unless they were already *in* a library? And if someone was here with us"— she looked around — "I guess we would know about it."

"So, now what?" said Arthur.

Francine sighed. "I wish I knew."

Chapter 8

• • • • • • • • • • •

The library had seemed dark before. Now somehow it seemed even darker. The rooms had seemed silent before. Now they seemed almost frozen in quiet.

Rinnggg!

"What's that?" asked Francine. She looked at Arthur.

"PHONE!" they said together.

They raced back to the main desk. The phone was still ringing.

Francine grabbed the receiver.

"Hello?"

"Hello, Ms. Turner," said the voice on the

line. *"This is Muffy Crosswire. I didn't get a chance to —"*

"Muffy!" Francine cut in. "It's me, Francine. Listen, I'm locked —"

"Oh, sorry, Francine, I must have dialed you by mistake. I meant to call the library. Ooops, can't talk now. I hear the bell for dinner. I'll talk to you later. Bye."

She hung up.

"Muffy! Wait! Muffy?" Francine stared at the phone.

"What did you do?" Arthur shouted. "How could you hang up on her?"

"I didn't hang up on her. She hung up on me. Anyway, I'm calling my mother, so relax."

Francine dialed her home number. She heard a *beep* and then a recording.

"We're sorry. To dial out of the library, you must enter the correct user code. Please hang up and try again."

"User code?" Francine stared at the phone. "But I don't know the user code."

She tried again anyway.

"We're sorry. To dial out of the library, you must enter —"

Francine slammed down the phone. "User codes! Passwords! What's this world coming to, anyway?"

"We're doomed," said Arthur.

"Oh, Arthur, just relax. You're such a wimp."

"Me? Well, you're a bossy, know-it-all . . . marshmallow."

"That does it, Arthur Read! If I have to spend the weekend here, I'm not spending it with you!"

She stormed out of the room.

"Fine with me," Arthur called after her. He looked around at the deepening gloom. "See if I care," he added softly.

Left to himself, Arthur looked around

for something to do. He picked up a magazine and started flipping through it. There was a picture of a roast turkey on one page.

Arthur's stomach grumbled.

"That sure looks good," he muttered. He ripped off part of the page and tried chewing it.

"Yuck!" he said, spitting it out. It didn't taste like turkey at all.

Thump!

What was that?

Thump!

Arthur frowned. Libraries were not supposed to make thumping noises.

"Francine?"

She didn't answer.

Arthur went back to the magazine. He wondered if the mashed potatoes and gravy would taste any better than the turkey leg.

Thump!

Arthur put down the magazine.

"Francine!" he called out.

The name echoed through the halls.

Where was she? Arthur started moving in the direction that Francine had gone.

"Francine! Francine! Where are you?"

Thump!

There it was again. And this time he also heard a girl screaming.

"Francine! Don't worry! I'm coming."

Arthur ran up the steps to the next level. He threw open the first door he came to.

It was a broom closet.

Arthur kept going. He heard more screaming coming from another door down the hall.

Arthur raced toward the door. He heard evil laughter coming from the other side.

There was no time to waste. Francine was in trouble! He took a deep breath — and burst in.

Chapter 9

• • • • • • • • • • •

As he entered the room, Arthur tripped on the rug and fell to the floor. His glasses flew off and sailed across the room.

They landed in the middle of a pizza box.

Arthur squinted and looked around.

"Francine, are you okay?"

Francine was sitting in a chair watching television.

"Of course I'm okay. Why wouldn't I be?"

Arthur scrambled across the floor and picked up his glasses. Strands of cheese dangled from the lenses.

Arthur wiped them off and put the glasses back on.

"I wasn't sure," he said. "I heard thumping."

"Oh, that . . . The movie I'm watching has monsters with big feet."

"And screaming!"

"Naturally. It's a horror movie."

"And evil laughing," Arthur went on.

"I know," said Francine. "The monsters have a strange sense of humor."

"So do you!" said Arthur. "When you didn't answer, I figured you were hurt or something. I was worried. I was coming to your rescue." He looked around. "Where are we, anyway?"

Francine shrugged. "It's the staff room, I think. I had no idea librarians were so well fed. I found the pizza in the refrigerator and zapped it in the microwave."

"Francine, let me get this straight. We're locked in the library. It's getting dark. We don't know how long we're going to be stuck here. And you're sitting here eating pizza and watching TV?"

She nodded. "I'll bet you had no idea I could be so resourceful."

That was true, but Arthur wasn't about to admit it. "Well, I only have one thing to say."

"And what's that?"

Arthur's stomach grumbled. "Were you planning to share?"

Francine considered it. "Why should I share with someone who calls me a marshmallow?"

"Look who's talking. You've got a pretty short memory. Remember when I got glasses? You called me four-eyes."

"Well, I . . . That's ancient history." She paused. "Hey, did you say you were coming to my rescue?"

"Sort of."

"You were, weren't you?" Francine

picked up another plate. "That was very brave of you, Arthur. Joan of Arc would be pleased." She paused. "Want some pizza?"

"Sure."

A little while later, Arthur and Francine sat back in their chairs.

"Ohhhh!" Arthur groaned.

"Double ohhhh!" said Francine.

The pizza was gone, and several empty packages of chips and cookies were scattered around.

Arthur smiled. "This is turning out better than I expected. No chores, no homework, no . . . D.W!"

He sat up in horror. His sister D.W. had suddenly appeared in the doorway.

"Hello, Arthur," she said. "You're in *big* trouble."

Just then, Arthur's father and Francine's mother came around the corner. Ms. Turner was with them.

"Arthur! Francine!" said Mr. Read.

"Thank goodness you're all right!" said Mrs. Frensky.

Ms. Turner shook her head. "I don't know how this could have happened. But I'm glad to see both of you children."

"Are you all right?" asked Mr. Read.

"Are you hurt?" asked Mrs. Frensky.

D.W. took a look around at the chips, the cookies, and the empty pizza box.

"Don't worry," she said. "I think they'll survive."

Chapter 10

● ● ● ● ● ● ● ● ● ● ● ●

Monday morning at school, everyone was crowding around to hear the full story.

"I've always thought," said Binky, "that the characters in books come out to play after the library closes. I don't suppose you saw any."

"Of course not," said Francine. "They're afraid of the ghosts."

"Ghosts!" said Buster. He shivered a little.

Francine nodded. "But they didn't bother us."

"Except for that one with no head," said Arthur. "Right, Francine?"

They winked at each other.

As the bell rang, the kids headed for their classrooms.

"So, who'd you do your report on?" Buster asked Arthur.

Arthur stopped short. Francine would have bumped into him, but she had stopped short, too.

"Report?"

Arthur and Francine exchanged a panicky look. In all the excitement, they had forgotten about Joan of Arc.

That look was still on their faces as Muffy finished her report a little while later. The blackboard was lined with Crosswire Motors charts and graphs.

"And so," she concluded, "it is no exaggeration to say that without Edward M. Crosswire, there would be no Elwood City as we know it."

"Very, um, illuminating, Muffy," said Mr. Ratburn. "That brings us to"— he looked down at his notes — "Arthur and Francine."

The two partners shuffled up to the front of the room. They stood before the class and cleared their throats.

"Um," said Arthur, "we picked Joan of Arc for our report. But we really didn't get a chance to learn as much as we could . . ."

"Because," Francine said suddenly, "we were too busy learning the true meaning of heroism. It isn't just the stuff you find in books. It's real life."

Arthur stared at her.

"That's right," Francine went on. "When we were locked in the library, it might have been really terrible. Actually, it was terrible at first, because we were fighting and everything. Then Arthur came to rescue me because he thought I was in danger."

"Exactly," said Arthur. "And Francine was really brave and resourceful, too. She found out where the food was. And saved me some pizza."

The class cheered.

"That's very good," said Mr. Ratburn. "It looks like your adventure taught you something important."

Arthur and Francine beamed at each other.

"So I'll give you until tomorrow to do your assignment."

"After all we've been through?" said Francine.

"Oh, yes," said Mr. Ratburn. "It should give your report special meaning."

Later that day, Arthur and Buster were walking home from school.

"I hate to say it," said Buster, "but Francine's not so bad."

Arthur nodded. "She can be a lot of fun. She's a good friend."

At that moment, Francine whizzed by

on her bike. She rode right through a puddle, splattering the boys with muddy water.

"Sorrryyy!" she yelled over her shoulder.

Arthur and Buster looked down at their wet shirts.

Arthur sighed. "But nobody's perfect," he said.